THIS **GRETCHEN**™ BOOK

BELONGS TO

Dedicated to Dick Chiara

GRETCHEN™
AND THE LOST CAROUSEL

illustrated by:
BARBI SARGENT

written by:
JOAN PHILLIPS

ART DIRECTION BY LEO BISSETT

Publishers • GROSSET & DUNLAP • New York

Gretchen was swinging up into the blue afternoon sky.

"I wonder if I can touch that apple blossom," she thought to herself. And the swing in the old apple tree went higher and higher.

Gretchen and all of her friends were playing in the meadow. Little Angela was trying to get into Charlie and Amy's tug-of-war game. And near the stream, Kristen was helping Peter wait for a shy turtle to come out of its shell.

"You have to be still, Peter," said Kristen. "We don't want to scare it away."

"I'm trying to be still," said Peter. "It's my feet that want to jump!"

Suddenly all of the children stopped playing and listened. Voices were coming from the nearby woods.

"Who can it be?" asked Amy.

"Let's go find out," grinned Charlie. "Maybe it's someone new we can play with!"

Gretchen led the way to the edge of the woods, and they all peered through the bushes.

A little pony was crying, "But I'm too tired to keep on looking."

A dappled gray mare and a white unicorn looked on, as a large black horse answered the little pony, "Please try, Rainbow. We just *have* to find it before the sun sets."

"What kind of horses are they?" whispered Amy.

"They don't look real, somehow," said Kristen.

"But they must be real," answered Gretchen. "They move and they talk."

At the sound of Gretchen's voice, Rainbow turned his head.

"Why, who are you?" Rainbow asked shyly.

"Oh, I'm Gretchen, and these are all my friends. But who are you? We've never seen horses that looked like you before."

"We are wooden carousel horses," said the dappled gray mare. "Usually we go round and round on our carousel, but once every year on Midsummer's Eve we come alive by magic and leave the carousel to wander in the forest."

Now the black horse continued the story in his deep voice, "But the next day we must return to the carousel before the sun sets and the evening star appears in the sky. That's when the magic ends. If we don't return by then, we will turn back to wood wherever we stand. If that ever happens, we will not be carousel horses anymore."

"But isn't it about time for you to be getting back?" asked Gretchen, glancing at the afternoon sky. "It is getting late."

"Yes, but that's just the problem," said the unicorn. "The carousel is not where we left it. It's gone."

"And we must find it before the evening star comes out," said the gray mare.

"Maybe we can help," suggested Peter.

"Yes," agreed Gretchen eagerly. "We can ask some animal friends if they have seen the carousel."

They found Gretchen's friend Barnabas singing in the branches of his favorite oak tree.

"Hello, Gretchen," chirped the bluebird. "You and your friends look awfully worried. What's wrong?"

Gretchen explained about the horses and the lost carousel.

"Have you seen it, Barnabas?" Charlie asked.

"Well, let me think," said Barnabas. "I did make a trip to the forest today, but I don't remember seeing a carousel. Sorry I can't help you."

"That's all right, Barnabas," said Gretchen. "Thanks for trying."

"Why don't you find Chester and ask him?" suggested Barnabas. "He gets a lot of news in town."

Chester the cat lived in the brick alley at the edge of town.
He and his friends were taking a nap in the sun, as usual.

"Hello, Gretchen. Hello, everyone," called Chester cheer-
fully. "What brings you all to town on such a beautiful
afternoon?"

"We're hoping you can help us," said Amy.

"Have you seen a carousel anywhere?" asked Charlie.

"So you want a carousel, do you?" said Chester, scratching his head slowly. "Well, the only one I know is kind of broken down now, but it has a lion to ride on, and a big striped zebra, and even a bear with a saddle…"

"Oh," sighed Gretchen, "that can't be the horses' carousel."

"Have you seen a carousel without any animals, Chester? asked Kristen.

"No animals?" said Chester. "I can't say that I've ever seen a carousel like that before."

"Thanks anyway," said Gretchen. "We'll just have to keep looking."

"Well, good luck," purred the cat, waving his paw until Gretchen and her friends were out of sight.

"What will we do now?" said Kristen, as they walked back toward the meadow. "It's getting late."

"I know," said Gretchen. "If we hurry, we can ask Penelope."

"Yes," said Charlie, "she's sure to have an idea."

Penelope the beaver swam to the bank of the bubbly creek and slapped her broad tail in delight at seeing Gretchen and her friends. SMACKA-WHACKY-WHOOSH!

"Howdy 'do! You're just in time for tea," said Penelope.

"I wish we could stay," said Gretchen, "but we have something terribly important to do. We have to find a lost carousel."

"You haven't seen one, have you, Penelope?" asked Peter.

"It's for the horses," piped up Angela.

Penelope wiggled her nose. "There aren't many carousels here at the bubbly creek," she said, laughing at the idea of a carousel for beavers.

"I'm afraid we won't be able to help the horses after all," said Amy sadly.

But just then they heard the sound of soft music floating over the trees.

"That sounds like carousel music now," said Penelope.

"You're right, it does!" said Charlie.

"Hurry," said Gretchen. "Let's go find it."

"Goodbye, Penelope," called the children, as they ran toward the music.

"Goodbye," chuckled Penelope. "Come back and have some tea another day!"

The music was coming from the far side of the woods. As they rounded the trees, the children gave a gasp of amazement. For there, sitting crosslegged, was the biggest person they had ever seen.

"Why, Gretchen," said the giant, "have you come to listen to my music?"

"Oh, it's you, Gargantuan," said Gretchen in surprise. "I didn't expect to see you today. Don't be afraid," Gretchen said to her friends. "Gargantuan won't hurt you, even if he *is* a little large!"

The giant chuckled and held out his hand. "Climb aboard," he said. "Come up and see my new music box."

"Where did you get that, Gargantuan?" Gretchen asked the giant breathlessly.

"Why, I found it early this morning. When I wound it up, it played the most wonderful tune. Don't you like it?" asked Gargantuan.

"But, Gargantuan," said Gretchen, "that isn't a music box! It's the horses' lost carousel!"

And then Gretchen told Gargantuan the whole story. The giant listened carefully, and when Gretchen finished, he asked, "Did you say the horses have to be back on the carousel by sunset?"

"Yes," everyone shouted.

When they saw the carousel, the horses sprang at once into their places. Rainbow was last because he had to slip into a little harness attached to a pretty blue pony cart.

"Come and ride," the gray mare called to the children.
"Oh, can we?" asked Amy, her eyes shining.
Kristen chose the unicorn, and Amy mounted the gray mare. Charlie wanted to ride Rainbow, so Gretchen helped Peter and Angela into Rainbow's pony cart and then climbed onto the black horse's broad back.

As the carousel ride began, the sky became streaked with the gold of the setting sun. Thanks to Gretchen and her friends, the horses were back on their carousel by sunset.

"Thank you, thank you," the carousel horses neighed to the children.

Just then Gretchen looked up at the sky and saw the evening
star come out. She felt the horse under her turn to wood, but
the carousel kept going round and round with the music.
   When the ride was over, Gargantuan put out his hand again.
"Come on up," he said, "and I'll see you home."

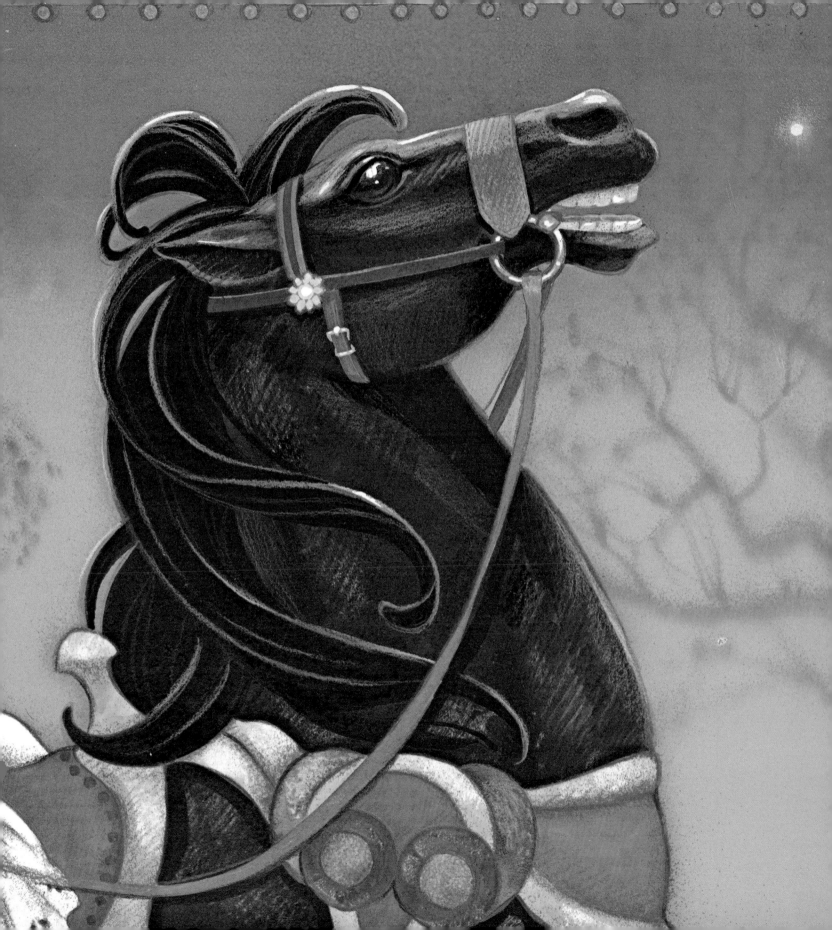

As the children scrambled over the giant's huge fingers, Gretchen looked up at him.

"Do you think we might meet Rainbow and the other horses again next year, Gargantuan?" she asked.

"Oh, yes. I think they know you are their friends," smiled the giant. "I'm sure they will look for you next year."

Gretchen looked over her shoulder and saw all of the horses going round and round on the carousel. She could hardly wait for next summer when the magic would bring them to life once more.